Star Friends
Wish Trap

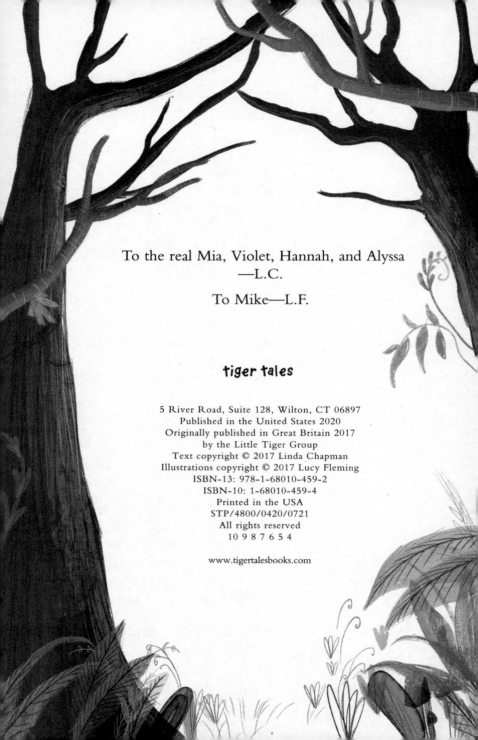

To the real Mia, Violet, Hannah, and Alyssa
—L.C.

To Mike—L.F.

tiger tales

5 River Road, Suite 128, Wilton, CT 06897
Published in the United States 2020
Originally published in Great Britain 2017
by the Little Tiger Group
Text copyright © 2017 Linda Chapman
Illustrations copyright © 2017 Lucy Fleming
ISBN-13: 978-1-68010-459-2
ISBN-10: 1-68010-459-4
Printed in the USA
STP/4800/0420/0721

www.tigertalesbooks.com

Star Friends

Wish Trap

BY LINDA CHAPMAN

ILLUSTRATED BY LUCY FLEMING

tiger tales

Contents

1

IN THE STAR WORLD

The meadows and mountains, hills and valleys all glittered with sparkling stardust. The animals who lived in the Star World were going about their business, but one snowy owl—Hunter—was watching something very important. In a pool, under a waterfall of stars, he could see what was happening in the human world.

He hooted softly: "Show me the Star Animals!" Peering curiously into the pool, he watched the images form, fade, and re-form.

First he saw a fox cub curled up on a bed

beside a girl with dark-blond hair. His muzzle was resting against her cheek, and she was rubbing his fur. Next, a squirrel scampering along the rail of a bunk bed, chattering to a girl with black curls. Then he saw a gentle deer being cuddled by a third girl with long, dark brown hair. In a fourth image, a wildcat was weaving between the legs of a girl with red hair and clever green eyes.

The owl nodded in satisfaction. Four of the young Star Animals who had recently made the journey from the Star World to the human world had found Star Friends. They would now teach those children how to use the magic that flowed between the Star World and the human world to do good deeds. Together, the Star Animals and their new friends would try to stop anyone using dark magic to cause unhappiness and hurt people. They would help keep the human world safe.

As the owl watched, the image in the sparkling pool changed again, this time showing a person in a hooded cloak holding up a glittering black pendant above a small, squat shape. The owl stiffened and gave an anxious squawk as he watched shadows swirl around the shape. Dark magic was happening! There was no doubt about it—someone was about to cause trouble near where the new Star Friends lived. Would the Star Friends and their animals realize? Would they be able to use their powers to stop the dark magic before people got hurt? He watched as the images continued to shift and change....

2
A Troubling Sight

Mia Greene lay on her bed with Bracken the fox cub snoozing in her arms. Rubbing his russet-red head, she felt her heart swell. It was hard to believe that she and Bracken had known each other for such a short time. But it was just two weeks and two days since she had seen him in the woods for the first time. Two weeks and two days since her life had changed forever.

Mia hugged Bracken closer. At first, she had thought he was just a young fox with unusual indigo eyes. But then he had spoken to her, and

she had found out that he was a Star Animal—a
magical animal from a faraway place called the
Star World.

Bracken's eyes blinked open. Seeing her
gazing at him, he tipped his head to one side.
"What are you thinking about, Mia?"

"When you first told me you were a Star
Animal," Mia told him softly.

Bracken wriggled into a sitting position. "You
should have seen your face when I first spoke to
you," he teased. "You looked really shocked."

"Of course I did. It was the first time anything magical had ever happened to me," said Mia.

Bracken licked her nose. "And now you're my Star Friend and know all about magic."

Mia nodded. It was amazing, and she could still hardly believe it. Every Star Animal who came to the human world had to find a child to be their Star Friend. Star Friends were able to hear and see the Star Animals because they believed in magic. Together, they used the magic that flowed between the human world and the Star World to do good and stop bad people who used dark magic to make others unhappy. Whenever Mia wanted to see Bracken, she could call his name and he would appear—but he was always careful to vanish when there were other people around.

Mia had been absolutely delighted when her best friends, Lexi and Sita, had also become Star Friends. Lexi's Star Animal was an energetic squirrel named Juniper, and Sita's was a gentle deer named Willow. They were all having a wonderful—if sometimes scary—time learning about magic together.

Bracken jumped off the bed and shook himself. "Why don't you practice your magic? The more you practice, the better you'll get at it."

"Okay," Mia said. Jumping up eagerly, she went to her desk with Bracken bounding around her legs. The desk's surface was covered with animal magazines, animal stickers, pens, pencils, and books. Pushing them to one side, she leaned forward, staring into her mirror.

One of the first things that Mia had learned when she started doing magic was that different Star Friends had different magical abilities. Her own magic had to do with sight. If she looked into a shiny surface, she could see things that were happening in other places. She could also see glimpses of the future, and Bracken had told her that if she kept practicing, she would be able to see into the past one day, too.

Focusing on the surface of the mirror, Mia let the rest of the world fade away and opened herself to the current of magic. It tingled through her body, making her feel like every inch of her skin was sparkling. What should she ask to see? She thought for a moment and then decided.

Show me the future. Show me something I need to see.

Her own reflection faded, and a picture of a girl appeared in the mirror. She was crouched on the ground, hugging her ankle and crying. Mia frowned. The girl seemed to be wearing the red and gray uniform of Mia's school, but Mia couldn't see her face. Who was she? What had happened to her?

I want to see more, Mia thought. But instead of the image becoming clearer, another image appeared. This time it was a different girl on a jungle gym. Mia couldn't see who it was, but she was swinging from the top bar by her hands. As Mia watched, she lost her grip, cried out, and fell.

Mia caught her breath as the girl hit the ground.

"What are you seeing?" Bracken asked curiously. Only Mia could see the images in the mirror.

"Two girls, in two separate images," Mia replied. "Both getting hurt. Wait, the image is changing again…."

Shock jolted through her as a new picture appeared—a skinny girl with shoulder-length black curly hair. She was staring at something that was coming toward her, and she looked terrified.

"It's Lexi!" Mia exclaimed, recognizing her friend.

The image disappeared, leaving Mia looking at her own reflection, her wide green eyes staring back at her and her dark-blond bangs falling across her face. She swung around. "There was something coming toward Lexi, and she looked really scared. Do you think she's okay?"

"Use your magic to find out," Bracken urged.

Mia turned back to the mirror. *I want to see Lexi wherever she is right now.*

A new image appeared in the glass—Lexi was in her bedroom, practicing handstands, her black curls brushing the floor. To Mia's relief, she looked just fine. A red squirrel with a fluffy tail and bright, inquisitive eyes was scampering along the top of the bunk bed.

Mia's breath rushed out. "It's okay. She's with Juniper in her bedroom."

"What did you ask the magic to show you when you saw those images?" Bracken said.

"I asked it to show me something in the future that I needed to see."

Bracken looked troubled. "Then the magic will have shown you those things for a reason.

Maybe they're going to happen because of dark magic." His ears flattened.

Mia stared at him. "You mean, you think there might be another Shade nearby?"

Bracken nodded, and Mia's heart beat a little faster. People who used dark magic could conjure horrible spirits called Shades from the shadows. The Shade would then either be set free to bring chaos and unhappiness wherever it went, or it could be trapped in an object and given to someone whom the person doing dark magic wanted to harm.

Mia had already encountered one Shade, which had been trapped in a makeup compact. It had talked to Cleo, her older sister, from within the little mirror, twisting her mind and making her feel jealous of her best friend. Thankfully, Mia, Lexi, and Sita had managed to defeat it and send it back to the shadows. But only with the help of another Star Friend, Violet.

Bracken padded around anxiously. "I think you should talk to the others. If there is another Shade, we must try and stop it."

"You're right. I'll get them to meet me at the clearing." Mia picked up her phone and typed in Lexi and Sita's names. After a moment's hesitation, she added Violet into the message, too.

She and Violet used to be friends when they were younger, but they didn't get along much at all now. Still, like it or not, Violet *was* a Star Friend and had helped send the last Shade back to the shadows. Mia had to include her. She tapped in her message.

> Need 2 talk 2 u all. It's important. C u at clearing in 45 mins. M x

She pressed Send.

3
MEETING UP WITH FRIENDS

Going downstairs, Mia heard Cleo calling out to their mom. "I'm going to babysit Paige for a few hours, Mom. I'll be back at seven."

"Okay," Mom said, coming to the kitchen door with Alex, Mia's little brother. "Say hi to Paige's mom and dad for me."

"I will," said Cleo.

"Train!" said Alex, spotting his model train by the bottom of the stairs. Mom put him down, and he toddled over to it.

Mia smiled at him. "Choo-choo!" She

pushed it across the floor and he followed it, giggling in delight.

Mia unhooked her coat from the pegs by the door. "I'm going out, too, Mom. Is that okay?"

"Where are you off to?" her mom asked.

"To the woods to meet up with Lexi and Sita. Violet might come, too." She'd already had texts back from Sita and Lexi saying they would meet her there, but she hadn't heard from Violet yet.

Her mom smiled. "So you and Violet are friends again now?"

"Um … kind of," Mia said, wondering what her mom would say if she told her the truth—that she was only including Violet because they were all Star Friends and could do magic.

Her mom looked happy. "I've always liked Violet. You were such good friends when you were little—always playing make-believe games about magic and animals. I'm glad you're becoming close again now that you're in the same class at school."

At the start of the school year, the teachers had shuffled the classes around. Sita and Lexi had been put in one fifth-grade class while Mia was in the other. As if being separated from her best friends wasn't bad enough, she had also ended up sitting next to Violet. Violet was really smart, but she was impatient and seemed to love pointing out any mistakes that Mia made. Violet didn't have many friends in the class and spent most of her lunchtimes reading.

"Why don't you have a sleepover next weekend and invite Violet, Sita, and Lexi?" Mom went on. "You could have a bonfire in the yard and toast marshmallows."

Mia wasn't sure that was a good idea— Lexi found Violet even more annoying than she did! But her mom was looking at her expectantly. "Okay, thanks, Mom. I'll ask the others," she agreed. "'Bye, Mom. 'Bye, Alex."

"Choo-choo!" said Alex, waving his train at her.

Mia shut the door behind her and zipped up her coat. Although the autumn sun was shining, there was little warmth in its rays, and the wind was blowing fallen leaves into piles.

As she wheeled her bike out from the garage, Mia caught sight of Cleo heading

down the street just ahead. Mia rode to catch
up with her.

"Oh, hi," said Cleo as Mia jumped off her
bike. "Where are you off to?"

"The woods by Grandma Anne's house," said
Mia.

"Again?" said Cleo in surprise. "Why
don't you all meet at home where it's
warm?" She shivered and dug
her hands into the pockets
of her coat.

"We like it there." Mia wished she could tell Cleo it was because of the Star Animals —it was where they had first appeared, and it was a particularly good place to do magic. It was private and overgrown and hardly anyone ever went there.

"Doesn't it make you feel sad—going past Grandma Anne's house all the time?" Cleo said curiously.

"Only a little bit," said Mia. Their grandma had died just over a month ago. At first Mia hadn't liked going near the house at all. But since she'd found out about the Star Animals, she'd started to feel differently. She suspected her grandma had been a Star Friend, too. Grandma Anne had always told Mia to believe in magic, and she had been very kind and helped so many people in town. Thinking that she might have been a Star Friend helped Mia feel close to her still.

Cleo sighed. "I really miss Grandma Anne.

Paige does, too. She was talking about her last time I babysat. I think it's harder for her— she's only seven." Paige was Grandma Anne's goddaughter and had been very close to her.

"Look, there's Paige," Mia said, pointing down the street.

Paige was bouncing on a trampoline in the front yard, turning effortless somersaults. Spotting them, she waved, and by the time they reached the driveway, she had scrambled off the trampoline.

"Hi." She grinned. Her brown hair was tied in two ponytails, and she had a smattering of freckles across her nose.

"Hi, Paige. I'll just go and tell your mom I'm here," said Cleo.

"Are you going to play with me, Mia?" Paige asked as Cleo headed into the house.

"I'm sorry, Paige, but I can't

stop today. I'm going to see my friends," said Mia.

"Are you seeing Lexi?" asked Paige eagerly. She and Lexi went to the same gymnastics studio, and Mia knew Paige really admired her.

She nodded. "I am."

"Say hi to her for me!" Paige said.

"Mia!"

Mia looked around. "You can say hi yourself," she said with a smile as she saw Lexi and Sita riding down the street toward them.

"Lexi!" Paige squealed in excitement.

Lexi and Sita got off their bikes, and Paige ran to give Lexi a hug.

"Hi, Paige," said Lexi.

"Do you want to see how good my backward walkover is getting?" said Paige. Without waiting for a reply, she put her arms over her head and dropped back into a bridge. "What do you think?" she said, the ends of her ponytails dangling down.

"That's really good, Paige," said Lexi.

"I've been practicing every day," said Paige
proudly as she flipped back to her feet. "I really,
really want to be on the competitive team like
you. I want it *so* much!"

"Keep on practicing and I bet you will be,"
said Lexi. "You're already third reserve."

Paige looked hopefully at her. "Do you
want to take a turn on the trampoline? We can
practice somersaults."

"We really should get going," said Mia, catching Lexi's eye. As she turned to leave, she noticed a pottery gnome tucked beside a nearby shrub. He was about as tall as her knees and had a little red hat, a green waistcoat, and the words "Make a Wish" on his brown belt.

"That's a cute gnome," Mia said. Paige patted his head. "One of Mom's friends gave him to us over the weekend. Mom's been trying to decide where to put him. I like him here by the trampoline. I've told him I really hope I get on the gym team!"

"I hope your wish comes true!" Lexi said, smiling at her.

They said good-bye and headed off. As they rode their bikes toward the clearing, Mia told them about the bonfire sleepover her mom had suggested.

"That sounds fun!" said Sita.

"There's only one catch," Mia said. "Mom wants me to invite Violet, too."

Lexi's face fell. "Do we have to?"

"Oh, Lexi, don't be mean," said Sita. "When we practiced magic together on Wednesday after school, she was fine."

"You mean except for saying she was surprised Mia couldn't see into the past yet? Oh, and telling me that she was glad she didn't have agility as her magic skill because doing stealth magic and being able to shadow-travel was much cooler?"

Sita frowned. "She didn't *exactly* say that. She just said she wouldn't want to run and jump and climb like you do. And when she was talking to Mia, I think she wanted to see if she could help."

"Mia doesn't need her help," said Lexi. "She's great at doing her magic."

Mia shot her friend a grateful look. It was wonderful that Lexi was so loyal, even if

Violet was right about the fact that she hadn't managed to see into the past.

"I don't think Violet means to be annoying," Sita said. "I think she wants to be friends, and she's trying to get us to like her. She just doesn't always go about it the right way."

"You can say that again," Lexi muttered. She caught Sita's eye and sighed. "Okay. I won't be mean, and I'll give her a chance. But I'd much rather it was just us—and I don't like that cat of hers at all."

Lexi was talking about Violet's Star Animal, a very smug wildcat named Sorrel.

"I know what you mean," Mia said. "I don't particularly want to invite Violet, but Mom really wants me to." She pushed the problem to the back of her mind. "I'll decide later. Right now, we've got other stuff to talk about."

"What sort of stuff?" said Lexi.

"Important magic stuff!" said Mia. "Come on!"

Putting their heads down, they pedaled as fast as they could to the clearing.

4
AN IMPORTANT MEETING

The town where Mia and her friends lived was called Westport, on the Pacific coast. Most of the town was on one side of the main road, set back in a maze of little streets. On the other side of the road were a few houses, as well as the woods that led to the clifftops, the beach, and the ocean.

Mia, Lexi, and Sita crossed the main street carefully and pushed their bikes onto a narrow, stony path with woods on both sides. Overhead, seagulls were circling in the gray sky. At the top of the road was a row of little houses with neat front yards. Farther down was Grandma Anne's little house and beyond that, the path led to the clifftop and the beach.

Mia glanced at the row of stone houses at the top of the road. Violet lived in the end one with her mom and dad. Mia thought about riding right past, but then she felt a pang of guilt. "Should we see if Violet's home? She might not have gotten my text."

Mia noticed there was no car in the driveway. Pulling out her phone, she checked it and saw that a message had just come through from Violet:

> Over at my grandma's. Will come and meet you as soon as I get back. V x

Mia hurried back to the others, feeling secretly relieved that it would just be the three of them and their Star Animals for a while. "She sent me a text—she's not home, but she says she'll meet us later."

They pedaled down the road, bumping over the potholes and trying not to skid on fallen leaves.

Leaving their bikes in Grandma Anne's yard, they pushed their way along the overgrown footpath that led to the clearing in the woods. Hearing the sound of the stream splashing up ahead, Mia's heart quickened in excitement. She sped up and burst into the clearing with Sita and Lexi at her heels. Instantly, Bracken the fox, Juniper the squirrel, and Willow the deer appeared.

Bracken spun in circles, yapping, Willow
cantered straight over to Sita, pricking her ears
in delight, while Juniper scampered up a nearby
tree trunk and leaped from branch to branch.

"Race me, Lexi!" Juniper chattered.

In a flash, Lexi was scrambling up the tree
after him. She was amazing at gymnastics
anyway, but when she drew on the current
of Star Magic, she could run and jump
and swing with amazing speed and skill.
She giggled as she chased after Juniper,
as agile as a squirrel herself.

Willow nuzzled Sita's hands while Bracken raced around Mia and stopped in a play bow, his bottom in the air and his tail waving. "I love being here!" he said.

Mia laughed. She knew she had to tell the others about what she'd seen in the mirror, but for a moment, she just wanted to enjoy herself. "Me, too."

Lexi grabbed a hazelnut from a bush and threw it gently at Mia. Her accuracy was right on, and it hit Mia's head. "Just getting some target practice in!" she said, grinning.

She somersaulted effortlessly down to the ground, but too late she realized that she had landed in a pile of nettles. "Ow!" she yelped.

"Don't worry," Sita called. "I'll help."

Lexi hobbled over, and Sita laid her hands on the nettle stings. Within a few seconds, the pain had cleared from Lexi's face.

"You made it better," Lexi said, examining her leg. The rash had vanished.

Sita grinned. She was still amazed by the way her healing abilities worked. "It's just like magic!"

Lexi chuckled and then ran toward Mia. "Tag!" she said, tapping Mia's shoulder and darting away.

Mia raced after her. She couldn't begin to match Lexi's speed, but she could use her magic to see where Lexi was heading. It was a strange feeling. When the magic was flowing through her, she just had to relax until she saw a shining outline appear around Lexi. The outline moved a split second before Lexi did, which meant Mia could sprint to the right place. "Got you!" she cried in triumph as her outstretched fingers touched Lexi's shoulder.

Lexi tagged her back in an instant and climbed a tree trunk.

"No going up trees!" called Sita who was watching with her arm around Willow's neck. "That's not fair to Mia."

Lexi dropped down and raced to the river, leaping confidently from one slippery rock to another. "Can't catch me, Mia!"

"Someone's coming!" called Sita in alarm.

In an instant, the three Star Animals vanished. Lexi and Mia swung around just as a girl with red hair came pushing through the Queen Anne's lace into the clearing. *Violet,* Mia realized with relief. A wildcat with a sleek tabby coat and slanted indigo eyes materialized at Violet's side. Bracken, Juniper, and Willow instantly reappeared, too.

"Sorry we're late," Violet said.

"Don't worry," said Sita, smiling. "We haven't done anything yet, really."

Sorrel, the wildcat, stalked forward. "I can see that. I would have thought you would have been practicing your magic *properly*."

"Just because the girls were having fun, doesn't mean they weren't learning more about their magic," Bracken protested. "They're … um…."

"Practicing teamwork," Juniper put in helpfully.

"That's it, practicing teamwork!" said Bracken.

"Hmm," Sorrel said disbelievingly. Sitting down, she flicked her tail around her paws. "Well, now that Violet and I are here, why doesn't Violet show you all how well she can shadow-travel? Violet's magical abilities are coming in leaps and bounds," she said smugly.

"Should I show you what I can do now?" Violet said eagerly, walking to a patch of shadows under an oak tree and looking at the others. "I've learned to use shadows to travel wherever I want. I just imagine where I want to go, and then I come out in the nearest patch of shadows by that place. Watch!" She stepped into the shadows and disappeared, appearing a few seconds later in another patch of shadows on the far side of the clearing. "Ta-da!" she said, grinning and holding up her hands. "Isn't that awesome?"

"That's great!" said Sita, clapping.

"Exceptional girl," purred Sorrel. "So talented."

Lexi rolled her eyes at Mia.

"What?" Violet said in surprise, catching the look. "Don't you two think it's good?"

"Yeah," said Mia, shrugging. "It's great, I guess." It *was* a cool thing to do, but did Violet really have to show off quite so much?

"I'll do it again," Violet said quickly, as if afraid she wasn't impressing them enough. "I'll go farther this time."

Bracken nudged Mia's hand. "Mia, you need

to tell the others what you saw in the mirror earlier."

"Oh, yes," Mia remembered. "Wait, Violet! There's something I really have to talk to everyone about. I saw some things when I was using my magic at home earlier—worrying things."

"Yes, let's listen to Mia," said Lexi, giving Violet a pointed look. "After all, that's why we came here. Not to watch you do magic."

Violet frowned. "I only wanted to show you because I think it's really important that we know each other's abilities—especially if we have to fight a Shade again one day."

"Violet's right," said Sita. "It is important, so we can work as a team. But right now, why don't we hear what Mia has to say? Let's sit down, and she can tell us what's going on."

As she listened to Sita's words, Mia felt her irritation melt away, and she found herself nodding in agreement. Sita's magic meant she was able to calm and soothe people and animals as well as heal them, and she was getting better at it all the time.

The tension vanished, and they all sat down on rocks and tree stumps. Mia quickly told them about the images she'd seen in the mirror. "The third image was of a girl with something coming toward her," she finished. She decided not to mention that it was Lexi in case it worried her friend. "She looked really scared."

"I wonder why you saw those things," said Sita.

"Mia asked the magic to show her what she needed to see," Bracken explained. "It must have shown her those images because they're important in some way in the future."

"Maybe, maybe not," Sorrel said with a shrug. "Everyone knows that looking into the future is a particularly difficult type of magic. Mia might just have gotten it wrong."

"I bet she didn't!" Lexi protested.

Willow jumped in quickly. "What do you think we should do, Bracken?"

"I think we should investigate," he said. "I'm worried that Mia saw those images because a Shade will make those things happen."

"Do we have to watch for creepy talking mirrors again?" said Sita with a shiver.

Willow shook her head. "The Shade could be trapped in any object."

"The deer is right," said Sorrel. "There are all different kinds of Shades —Nightmare Shades, Ink Shades, Wish Shades. Some live in mirrors and talk to people and make them do bad things, like that Mirror Shade. Others can bring bad luck or trap people in different ways."

"Are Shades controlled by the person who conjured them?" Violet asked.

"No," said Sorrel. "A Shade can be trapped but not controlled. Someone using dark magic can choose which type of Shade best suits their evil purposes. Then they trap them in an object and put it in someone's possession. If a Shade is not trapped, they will be free to affect whomever they like."

"But who would trap a Shade—and why?" said Sita.

"Someone who wanted to cause trouble," said Sorrel darkly.

"What should we do?" said Lexi.

"Well, if you all really think we need to

take these visions seriously, we should try and find out if any dark magic has been used," said Sorrel. "As you all know, I am excellent at sniffing out Shades."

"Willow can sniff out Shades, too," Lexi pointed out.

"Not as well as Sorrel," admitted Willow.

Just as humans had different abilities with magic, Star Animals also had different abilities, and some of them were more sensitive to dark magic than others.

"I know, Sorrel! Why don't you and I shadow-travel around to see if you can detect a Shade anywhere in town?" Violet suggested.

Mia nodded in agreement. "Good plan."

Violet jumped to her feet.

"Wait!" said Lexi quickly. "That's too dangerous. What if you do find a Shade and get into a fight with it?"

"There won't be a fight," said Violet. "I'm a Spirit Speaker, remember? If I meet a Shade,

I can just command it to go back to the shadows."

Sorrel rubbed her head against Violet's hand. "Your bravery is admirable, Violet. But it may not be that simple. Remember what I have told you—you need a Shade to look you in the eyes before you can command it, and you need to be in full control of your magic."

"Don't go off on your own, Violet," said Sita. "The Mirror Shade was horrible."

"Sita's right," said Lexi. "I think we should wait and see what happens. If there is a Shade nearby, then strange things will start to happen. When they do, we can come up with a plan."

"No! I think we should try and stop bad things *before* they happen. We should do something right now." Violet turned impatiently to Mia. "Mia, you agree with me, don't you?"

Mia remembered the image she had seen of Lexi looking terrified. She desperately wanted to stop that from happening, but she didn't think Violet should really go rushing off on her own, and she also didn't want to hurt Lexi and Sita's feelings by siding with Violet. Maybe Sorrel was right, and the images she had seen weren't going to come true. "Umm…." She glanced around. "Well, maybe we don't need to do anything just yet."

Violet frowned. "You don't really think that."

"Yes, she does," said Lexi, linking arms with Mia. "And Sita agrees with us, too. Don't you, Sita?"

Sita gave a nod.

Sorrel glared at Bracken. "Come on, fox. You know we need to act. Persuade your human to change her mind."

Bracken pressed against Mia's legs. "Whatever Mia wants, I'm happy with."

"It's decided then," said Lexi quickly. "If a Shade is doing things, it will become obvious, and we can make a plan then. In the meantime, we just wait."

Violet's mouth tightened as she looked at the three of them standing together. "Fine. I'm going home."

"Violet—don't," said Sita, holding out her hand.

But Violet ignored her. She walked toward a shadow at the edge of the clearing, and Sorrel leaped after her. As soon as Violet's feet touched the shadow, she vanished. Sorrel hissed at the others and then vanished, too.

"Why does Violet have to be a Star Friend?"

Lexi cried in frustration.

"We shouldn't have upset her," said Sita.

"All we did was vote against her plan," said Lexi. "There was no need for her to go off in a big huff."

Mia felt torn. She couldn't stop thinking about the image of Lexi and wondering if she should have sided with Violet. What if the things she had seen *were* accurate, and something horrible happened to her friend? What if it turned out she could have done something to stop it? An icy finger ran down her spine.

Juniper leaped from Lexi's shoulders, ran to a nearby tree, and raced up the trunk. "Let's not just stand around. We should make the most of the time that's left."

"Juniper's right," said Lexi. "Let's practice our magic. If we do end up fighting a Shade again, we'll need our magic to be as strong as possible. The more we practice, the better we'll get."

She charged after Juniper and climbed
the tree. She swung onto a high branch and
dropped down, so she was dangling from her
hands, then she swung along the branch like a
monkey.

Sita went to the base of the tree and repaired
the stems of a clump of ferns that had been
squashed in the earlier game of tag.

Bracken nudged Mia's hand with his nose.
"Are you going to practice your magic, too?"

She sighed. "I don't really feel like it."
Kneeling down, she wrapped her arms around
him and hugged him tightly. He licked her
cheek comfortingly.

Please let Lexi be okay, Mia thought as she
watched Lexi drop down from the branch and
cartwheel effortlessly across the grass. *Please let
the vision I saw be wrong.*

5
SECRETS

When the sun started to set, the girls went to get their bikes from Grandma Anne's yard. A slim, gray-haired lady was pruning the rose bush beside the front door.

"Aunt Carol!" Mia said, waving.

The elderly lady looked around. "Hello, Mia. I thought I'd stop by and clean up the yard for your mom and dad."

"That's really kind of you," Mia said. Aunt Carol had been one of Grandma Anne's closest friends.

Lexi and Sita picked up their bikes. "You two go on," Mia told them. "I'll stay with Aunt Carol for a while."

"Okay. See you tomorrow," Sita said, and she and Lexi biked away up the road.

"So, how are you?" Aunt Carol asked Mia.

"Good, thanks. How about you, Aunt Carol?"

"Oh, I've been keeping myself busy," Aunt Carol replied. "I'm helping with the Bonfire Night event in the ballfield next week. I've also been cleaning up the town square and doing some knitting for the town carnival."

"Grandma Anne used to do all those things," Mia said, feeling a flicker of sadness.

"I know," Aunt Carol said. "I've never really got involved before, but now that she's no longer with us, I thought I should step in and help. I have to say, I'm really enjoying it." Clipping her pruning shears shut, she sat down on a bench in front of the house. She patted it, and Mia sat down beside her.

"When I saw you a few weeks ago, you told me about a young fox with indigo eyes that you'd seen in the woods. Have you seen him again?"

Mia hesitated. The Star Animals were a secret, but surely it was okay to say she'd seen him again. "Actually, I have. Quite a few times."

"And...?" the elderly lady prompted.

"And what?" said Mia, puzzled.

Aunt Carol dropped her voice. "Have you discovered his secret?"

Mia stared. *Secret?* Aunt Carol couldn't know about Star Animals, could she? Bracken had said there weren't any other Star Animals in the area, so she knew Aunt Carol couldn't be a Star Friend.

Aunt Carol leaned even closer. "Have you discovered that he's a Star Animal, Mia?"

Mia's mouth fell open in surprise.

Aunt Carol chuckled as she saw the shock on her face. "It's all right, my dear. I know all about Star Animals—your grandma was a Star Friend. Did you know that?"

"No … but … but I thought she might have been," stammered Mia. "Are you a Star Friend, too?"

Aunt Carol shook her head. "I always wanted to be, but I was never lucky enough to meet a Star Animal. Once when we were about the same age as you, I showed up at your grandma's house unexpectedly and saw her with her Star Animal—she was a silver wolf."

Mia caught her breath. A silver wolf! Grandma Anne had always loved wolves— her house had been full of wolf pictures and ornaments. That explained why!

"Your grandma explained to me about Star Animals and swore me to secrecy," Aunt Carol went on. "She would tell me about her magic adventures and, when I got a little older, I learned that you didn't need to be a Star Friend to do magic. I found out how to use crystals to channel magic to heal and help people." She patted Mia's hand. "Your grandma and I worked together over the years. Now that you're a Star Friend, I'd like to do the same with you, too."

Mia was at a loss for words. Part of her was really excited at the thought of talking to Aunt Carol about magic. But she had promised Bracken she wouldn't mention the Star World to anyone who wasn't a Star Friend. She hesitated. If Aunt Carol knew about it already, and if Grandma Anne had trusted her, then surely it would be fine if she did, too, right?

"Would you like my help?" Aunt Carol's eyes twinkled.

Mia smiled. "Yes, please!"

"So the fox is your Star Animal?" asked Aunt Carol.

"His name is Bracken," Mia said. "Lexi, Sita, and Violet are Star Friends, too."

"You lucky, lucky girls," said Aunt Carol. "Have you learned about your magical abilities yet?"

Mia nodded. "My abilities have to do with sight."

"Interesting," said Aunt Carol thoughtfully. "Your grandma's abilities had to do with healing. Are you finding it easy to use your magic?"

"Sort of," said Mia. "Although I'm no good at seeing the past yet. I have seen some things from the future, but I'm not sure if they're accurate."

"Very few people see the future clearly when they first start using magic," said Aunt Carol.

Mia felt relieved. It would be much better if the things she'd seen weren't really going to happen.

"If you want to improve, you need to try really hard," Aunt Carol advised. "You have to concentrate on forcing the magic to work for you. That's what works for me when I do magic."

Mia frowned. "But Bracken told me not to try and force the magic. He said it would work better if I relax."

"That's only at first," said Aunt Carol. "When you get used to doing it, you have to really focus on what you want to achieve."

"Oh, okay," said Mia. "Thank you."

Aunt Carol patted her hand. "Do you know much about dark magic yet?" she asked.

"We had to fight a Shade last week." Mia explained about the Shade in the mirror. "And now Bracken thinks there might be another Shade nearby because I saw some horrible things happening when I asked the magic to show me the future."

"Oh, my dear. Please don't worry too much. Your visions probably aren't accurate at the moment." Aunt Carol gave Mia a kind smile. "I can't tell you how many times I got things wrong when I first started seeing into the future. It would be really unusual to have to face another Shade so soon unless someone was conjuring them up from the Shadows on purpose. But I'm sure that's not happening in Westport. To put your mind at ease, how about I use my crystals to check? I'll soon find out if there's anything strange going on."

"That would be great. Thank you!" Mia felt as if a weight had been lifted from her shoulders. If Aunt Carol could check to see if there was a Shade, then there was no need to feel worried that they weren't doing anything. Hopefully Aunt Carol was right, and her visions weren't going to come true.

She wondered what the others would say when she told them that Aunt Carol knew all about magic.

"Good girl." Aunt Carol's warm blue eyes met hers. "Remember, if you ever need advice about magic, you can always ask me."

Mia hugged her happily. "I will. Thank you so much, Aunt Carol! Thank you!"

6
A WORRISOME TIME

Mia biked quickly all the way home. As soon as she got there, she ran to her bedroom, shut the door, and whispered Bracken's name.

Bracken appeared in the middle of her rug and put his paws on her knees. "You're excited," he said, his tail wagging.

"I *am*." Mia threw herself down on the rug and told him all about Aunt Carol. "Oh, Bracken, she knew about the Star World. Grandma Anne *was* a Star Friend. She told Aunt Carol about it. Aunt Carol said she can do magic with crystals and stuff—she and Grandma Anne used to work together."

Bracken flattened his ears, a troubled look on his face. "Oh."

"What's the matter?" Mia asked.

Bracken paced around. "Mia, people who aren't Star Friends aren't supposed to know about Star Animals. We were told when we came here that it was really important that the Star World was kept secret."

"But Aunt Carol's really nice. She says she would have loved to be a Star Friend, but she never got the chance," said Mia.

Bracken still looked anxious, so Mia petted him. "Please don't worry. Grandma Anne wouldn't have told Aunt Carol if she couldn't trust her. She gave me some tips on how to make my magic work better, and she's going to see if she can find out if any dark magic is being used nearby." She tickled Bracken under the chin where his fur was really soft and fluffy. "Don't worry. Aunt Carol is good—I know she is."

Bracken licked her cheek. "If you trust her then I do, too."

Mia remembered something else. "Aunt Carol said the same thing as Sorrel—that the things I saw in the future might not be accurate because I'm just beginning to learn how to use my magic," she said. "Maybe all those things I saw aren't going to happen and I just got it wrong." She looked at him hopefully.

Bracken rubbed his paw with his nose. "Maybe."

"And if it does turn out that there is a Shade after all, we'll stop it," declared Mia.

"Definitely!" Bracken agreed.

Putting her arms around him, Mia felt a rush of happiness—when she was hugging Bracken, everything was all right with the world.

"Aunt Carol knows about Star Animals and can do magic?" Sita echoed at recess the next day.

"Yes, she uses crystals to do magic!" Mia said. She, Violet, Sita, and Lexi were in a quiet spot at the far end of the playground, away from the school, where there was a grassy bank ending in a low wall. Two of the girls from Lexi's gymnastics team—Hannah and Alyssa—were taking turns walking along the wall as if it was a balance beam. Mia and the others were standing a little ways off, keeping their voices down.

Violet had barely spoken to Mia, Lexi, and Sita when they had gotten to school that morning. She was clearly still annoyed with them, but the news about Aunt Carol was much too interesting for her to resist. Now she joined the others as they crowded around

Mia, the argument forgotten.

"I can't believe this! What did she say about your visions?" Violet demanded.

"That they're probably not going to come true," Mia whispered in relief. "She said she'll try to find out whether there is a Shade so we don't need to do anything for now. She'll use her crystals and—"

She was interrupted by a scream.

They swung around just in time to see Hannah crashing to the ground. She cried out in pain. For a fleeting second, Mia thought she saw something red and green racing through the bushes—but she didn't have time to look closely. Hannah needed help.

"My ankle!" Hannah gasped.

"I'll get a teacher!" said Alyssa, sprinting off.

Sita crouched beside Hannah and touched her shoulder. "It's okay, you'll be all right," she said soothingly. "What happened? Did you lose your balance?"

"No. Someone pushed me!" Hannah said through her tears.

"Pushed you?" echoed Violet.

"Yes," said Hannah. "I felt a shove."

"But there wasn't anyone near you," said Lexi.

"I felt it," Hannah insisted. Tears rolled down her cheeks. "What am I going to do? If my ankle's hurt, I won't be able to do gymnastics."

Lexi, Violet, and Mia all glanced at Sita. Mia
was sure the others were thinking the same as
her. Could Sita heal Hannah? But Sita gave a
small shake of her head, motioning with her
eyes to the crowd of children beginning to
gather. She couldn't risk healing Hannah in
front of them.

Miss Harris came hurrying through the
crowd. "Out of the way, everyone! Out of the
way!"

She shooed Mia and the others back and
crouched down beside Hannah, assessing
her ankle. "Oh, Hannah. I think it might
be broken," she said. "I'm going to call an
ambulance." She pulled out her phone.

Mia felt a tap on her arm. It was Paige.
The younger girl's eyes were wide. "What
happened?" she whispered.

"She fell off the wall," Mia said. She
remembered what Hannah had said about
being pushed, but there had been no one

anywhere near. She must have imagined it
... or maybe she made it up because she was
embarrassed about falling. She was the best
gymnast on the team.

"Is she going to be okay?" Paige asked.

"Miss Harris thinks her ankle might be
broken," said Mia.

Miss Harris stood up. "Okay, everyone. Go
back to your classrooms, please."

As Mia followed the crowd back into
school, she turned and looked over her
shoulder. Hannah was on the ground still,
hugging her injured ankle. Mia stopped dead,
feeling shock run through her. It was the first
image she'd seen in the mirror the day before!

"Mia?" Sita looked at her. "Are you all
right?"

Mia shook her head. "No," she whispered.

"What is it?" said Sita.

"When I was looking into the future
yesterday, I saw someone on the ground

holding her ankle—it was Hannah! I know it was!" The other images flashed through her mind—a girl falling from a jungle gym, Lexi looking terrified.... Her blood turned to ice. "Oh, Sita—what if the things I saw *are* going to come true after all?"

7
TROUBLE!

School felt like it was never going to end. All day, Mia kept thinking about the fact that the first vision she'd seen in the mirror had come true. News came back from the hospital after lunch that Hannah *had* broken her ankle. She wouldn't be able to do gymnastics for a couple of months.

The girls met in the playground after school.

"We have to talk," Mia told the others. "In private."

"Should we ask if we can go down to the

beach?" asked Violet. Now that there were important things to discuss, she seemed to have completely gotten over her huff from the day before. "We could say we have to collect some shells for a project. There'll hardly be anyone there at this time of year."

"I'm supposed to be going to gymnastics," said Lexi. "But I could try telling my mom I'm too upset because of Hannah."

"Let's ask," said Mia.

They all ran off. Luckily their moms and dads agreed to them going to the beach provided they took their phones and were home before it got dark.

Leaving their bags and lunchboxes with their parents, they hurried through town, crossed the street, and headed down the road. They passed Grandma Anne's house and went on to where the road ended in a small parking lot on the clifftop. It was a very blustery day with the sun only occasionally shining out from behind fast-moving, pale-gray clouds. The cold, salt-filled breeze whipped their hair around their faces, and seagulls shrieked as they were tossed around by the wind.

"Come on," Mia said, heading down the stony path that led to the beach. The tide was out, and the beach was deserted except for a couple of dog walkers in the distance.

"It's hard to hear!" Sita shouted above the wind as they stepped onto the beach.

"Let's go to the base of the cliff," said Lexi. "It'll be more sheltered there."

They found a natural hollowed-out space with dry stones to sit on at the bottom of the cliff. They sat down, the cliff shielding them from the wind. "Do you think it's safe to call the Star Animals?" said Mia. She really wanted to talk to Bracken.

Violet nodded. "No one usually comes this far down the beach. And if someone does come, they can always vanish."

They all whispered their Star Animal's
name, and Bracken, Sorrel, Juniper, and Willow
instantly appeared.

"Are you all right?" Bracken said, cuddling
into Mia's side. "You look worried."

"There was an accident at school," she told
him. They filled the animals in about what had
happened to Hannah.

"I wish I could have helped her," said Sita.
"But there were too many people around."

"Maybe you could help heal her now," said

Bracken eagerly.

Sorrel sighed. "The child has a broken ankle, fox. Doctors have seen her. Do you not think that the adult humans will ask questions if it miraculously heals?"

Bracken looked crestfallen. "Oh. I suppose so."

Mia put her arm around Bracken and pulled him close to her. "Listen, everyone. When I looked into the future yesterday, I saw Hannah after she'd hurt herself. I didn't know it was Hannah then because I couldn't see her face, but now I know that the things I saw yesterday are coming true."

"Well, technically only *one* of them has come true," Sorrel said.

"If one has come true, the others might, too," said Mia. *Like the vision with Lexi in it*, she added in her head.

"Why don't you try again and find out what you see today?" said Bracken.

Mia pulled a small, round mirror out of her pocket. She'd found it in the drawer of her desk the night before—Grandma Anne had given it to her a few years ago.

"Wait!" said Sorrel, leaping over to her. "I should check it to make sure there is no dark magic." She sniffed the mirror. "It's fine," she declared.

Mia took a breath and, cradling the mirror in her hands, she stared into it, opening herself to the magic current. She remembered Aunt Carol's advice. If she wanted her magic to work well, she had to really concentrate.

Reveal the future to me, she commanded in her head.

A faint image appeared in the mirror. She stared hard at it, but the more she tried to focus on it, the more indistinct it became.

Frustration welled inside her. "My magic's not working correctly. I can't see the future."

Bracken licked her hand. "Why don't you

try to see what is happening somewhere else right now? That might be easier."

Mia sighed. "Okay." She looked back into the mirror. *Show me something important that's happening right now*, she thought.

The surface of the mirror shivered, and a picture appeared. It was Alyssa playing on her jungle gym, climbing up to the top.

Fear gripped Mia. No! It was like the image she'd seen before. Only when she'd seen it yesterday, it had been in the future, and she hadn't been able to see who it was. Now it was happening for real. "Oh, no," she breathed.

"What is it?" demanded Violet.

Mia didn't answer. She was too busy watching Alyssa, grabbing the top bar of the jungle gym with her hands and dangling happily. As she did so, there was a blur of color above her, and then suddenly Alyssa cried out, snatching one hand away from the bar as if she'd been burned. She dangled precariously from her other arm.

"Alyssa!" gasped Mia as she watched her lose her grip and fall....

"What's happening, Mia?" demanded Lexi.

Mia saw Alyssa tumble to the grass. She lay there for a few seconds before sitting up and starting to cry. She was cradling her wrist to her chest.

Mia looked up at the others. They were all staring at her.

"What is it?" said Sita. "What did you see?"

Mia managed to get out an explanation of what she had seen in the mirror. "It's Alyssa. It looks like she's hurt her wrist," she finished.

Sorrel hissed. "Two girls hurt in one day. This is too much of a coincidence. I'm beginning to think you might be right, fox, and that there really must be a Shade involved."

Violet got to her feet. "Sorrel, why don't you and I shadow-travel to Alyssa's house and see if we can find any trace of one?"

"But what if someone sees you?" Sita said uneasily.

"We'll be careful. And we can't just sit around doing nothing." Violet pushed her hands through her hair. "We're Star Friends, and we're supposed to stop dark magic if it's happening!"

All Mia could think about was her third vision—the one where Lexi had been looking terrified. What if that came true, too? "I think Violet's right—she and Sorrel should go."

Lexi looked anxious. "I think it's too dangerous. It would be better to go and talk to Aunt Carol again and see if she's discovered anything."

"Mia could do that while Sorrel and I go shadow-traveling," said Violet impatiently.

"Good idea," said Bracken.

"Not a good idea but an excellent one," said Sorrel, weaving through Violet's legs.

The sun came out briefly, casting a patch of shadows at the foot of the rock. Violet stepped into it. "Sorrel and I won't do anything except try and sense if a Shade is involved," she said. "I'll let you know what we find out tomorrow. Come on, Sorrel."

With that, they vanished.

Mia chewed her bottom lip. If her visions had been right, then Lexi would be in danger next.

Bracken nuzzled her. "Don't worry, Mia," he said, seeming to read her thoughts. "We'll soon find out what's going on."

8
THE PLAN

After saying good-bye to the animals, Mia, Lexi, and Sita made their way back across the beach and up the road. Lexi and Sita continued on home, while Mia went to Aunt Carol's house. When she got there the lights were off, but there was smoke coming from the chimney, which suggested someone was home. She knocked on the door, but there was no answer.

Mia groaned inwardly and wished she could shadow-travel like Violet—then she could go to wherever Aunt Carol was.

Just as she reached her house, her phone buzzed. Glancing at the screen, Mia saw a text from Violet.

> Def a S at A's. We need to talk. Can u get to schl early 2moro? V x

Mia's heart sank. For a moment she had a flashback to when they had been fighting the Mirror Shade and it had injured Bracken with its sharp, knife-like fingers. Were they going to have to fight another Shade?

She typed a quick reply.

> See u 8:30 at schl. Tell the others. M x

Slipping the phone into her pocket, she opened the front door. As she stepped inside, she heard voices in the kitchen. Hope flared inside her. Was it Aunt Carol?

But as she reached the kitchen door, she saw that it was Paige and her mom. Paige was playing trains with Alex on the floor, while her mom was having a cup of tea.

"Hi, sweetheart," Mom said to Mia. "Did

you get the shells you needed?"

"Shells?" Mia remembered they were supposed to have been collecting shells on the beach. "Oh, yes, shells!" she said quickly. "Yep, we got everything we needed."

"These school projects," said Mom to Paige's mom. "There's always something else for them to do or find, isn't there?"

"Tell me about it," said Paige's mom with a groan.

"Mi-Mi!" Alex said, holding up a train to Mia.

"Here's another tunnel, Alex," said Paige, lifting her leg so Alex could push a train underneath.

Just then, Paige's mom's phone buzzed. "Oh, no," she said as she checked the message.

"What is it?" Mom asked in concern.

"You know Alyssa who goes to gym with Paige? She's fallen off her jungle gym."

Paige swung around. "Is she hurt?"

"I'm afraid so." Her mom nodded as she reread the message. "Her mom says she sprained her wrist. She's going to be out of gymnastics for at least a month."

"No!" Paige's hand flew to her mouth. "And Hannah hurt herself today, too." Her eyes filled with tears.

Poor Paige, Mia thought. Two of her friends getting hurt in one day. *We've got to stop this Shade.* She gave Paige a sympathetic look.

"I heard about Hannah," Mom said. "She broke her ankle, didn't she?"

Paige's mom nodded. "That's two members of the gymnastics team down. You're going to be in the competition at this rate, Paige."

Paige gave a sob. "I don't want to be in it

just because people are getting hurt." She ran to her mom.

"Oh, Paigey." Her mom hugged her. "Don't cry. Your friends will be okay. They'll just be out of gymnastics for a while."

"It's a bit of a coincidence that they're both on the team, isn't it?" said Mom, shaking her head.

Mia felt like someone had just tipped a bucket of icy water over her head. Was it a coincidence that two girls on the team had both had accidents? Or was it *because* they were on the team?

"I'm just going upstairs," she said, heading to the door. She needed to talk to Bracken right away!

The moment she reached her bedroom, she shut the door and called Bracken's name. As soon as he appeared in front of her, she burst out, "Oh, Bracken. I had a horrible thought."

She sat down on the bed and told him. "What if someone's trying to hurt people on the team?" she finished.

"But who would do that?" said Bracken.

"I don't know," Mia said. "The team wins a lot of competitions. Maybe … maybe someone on one of the other teams wants to try and stop them." She hugged him. "Bracken, if I'm right, Lexi could be in real danger. The Shade might be after her next."

Bracken nuzzled her cheek. "Don't worry. We'll find out what's going on and stop it."

Mia buried her face in his soft fur. "We have to!" she whispered.

The girls met on the playground before school. Mia was desperate to tell the others that she suspected the Shade was targeting the gymnastics team, but she didn't want to upset Lexi. And what if she was wrong?

Luckily, Violet took charge. Looking like she could hardly contain her excitement, she dragged them over to the wall.

"Okay, so last night this is what happened," she whispered to them. "Sorrel and I shadow-traveled to Alyssa's yard, and Sorrel smelled that a Shade had been on the jungle gym. For sure. Sorrel said it was a really strong smell. So then we decided to come here—to school — and Sorrel smelled the same scent here, too. Somehow *the same Shade* caused both Hannah and Alyssa's accidents!"

"What do we do?" Sita said.

"We need to find out what type of Shade it is," said Violet.

"And how it caused the accidents," said Lexi.

"And what object it's trapped in," added Violet. She glanced at Mia. "You're being quiet today."

"I'm just thinking about it all," Mia said. She glanced around at the busy playground. She wanted to wait until Bracken and the other animals were there before they figured out how to find out more about the Shade. "I think we should go to the clearing after school."

Lexi nodded. "I was wondering if you could use your magic to try and look back at the accidents—you might be able to see how the Shade caused them."

"Great idea!" said Violet.

Lexi looked surprised at the praise.

"All of you ask if you can come to my

house after school," Violet went on. "We'll go to the clearing, and Mia can use her magic."

Sita nodded. "Then maybe we'll find out what's going on."

To Mia's relief, nothing happened to Lexi that day at school. She decided she would tell the others about the third vision when they got to the clearing and could talk about it properly, with the Star Animals there, too. She watched the clock, willing the school day to be over.

"What? You four want to meet up *again?*" Mia's mom said when Mia ran over to her on the playground and asked if she could go to Violet's house. "Don't you see enough of each other in school? Well, okay, I guess. Be back by dinnertime, though." Mia nodded. "Now, did you ask everyone if they want to sleep over tomorrow night? Should I have a quick word with their parents?"

"Oh." With everything that had happened, Mia had completely forgotten about the sleepover. "I … um … asked Lexi and Sita," she said. "They can come."

"And Violet?" Mom asked.

"I haven't asked her yet," Mia admitted.

"Her dad's over there. I'll go and ask him." Mom headed off, and Mia went to join Violet and Sita.

"Mom said it's fine for me to go to your house," said Mia. "Also, I'm going to have a sleepover at mine tomorrow," she said to Violet. "Do you want to come?"

Violet's face lit up. "A sleepover? Yes, please!"

Mia felt guilty about not mentioning it sooner. Violet hadn't been nearly as annoying the last few days. She'd even been nicer in class. Maybe Sita had been right about her just really wanting to be friends.

Lexi came running over. "Mom says I can be out for an hour but then she's going to pick me up because I've got a piano lesson and she won't let me miss it. Come on. Let's go."

They dumped their bags at Violet's house, grabbed a bag of chips and an apple each, and then set off down the road toward the clearing.

"Okay, I've been thinking about the accidents and what we can do…," Violet began.

"Shh," said Mia, spotting a woman riding up the hill toward them on a big gray horse.

Violet lowered her voice so the rider couldn't hear. "The most important thing is to find out what object the Shade is trapped inside. Then we can try and get a hold of it and—"

Before she could finish her sentence, they heard the horse rider shout out. Looking up, they saw the horse rearing up on its back legs. The rider grabbed for the reins, but as she struggled to keep control of the horse, she lost her balance and fell to the ground. The horse bolted toward the girls at a gallop.

"Watch out!" yelled Violet. She grabbed Sita and Mia, who were on either side of her, and pulled them to the side of the road.

To Mia, it seemed as if time had slowed down. The horse's hooves clattered on the

stones, its nostrils flaring as it thundered up the road. Mia thought she caught sight of a flash of red and green in the bushes at the side of the road, but she only registered it for a second before she realized the horse was galloping right at Lexi.

"Lexi!" gasped Mia as she saw her friend's eyes widen in fear.

9
THE WORK OF A SHADE

Mia felt magic rush through her. She saw the
horse's glowing outline starting to swerve
to the right to avoid Lexi but at that exact
moment, Lexi made a move the same way to
try and get out of its path.

"Go the other way, Lexi!" shrieked Mia.

Lexi's magic must have been coursing
through her, too. In the blink of an eye, she had
thrown herself to the other side, somersaulted
in the air, and jumped to her feet, unhurt.

The horse swerved just as Mia had seen it

would. It stumbled and regained its balance,
then slowed and came to a stop. It stood
trembling at the side of the road, its sides
heaving. Sita ran over to it and took its reins.
She touched the horse's neck and whispered to
it. Mia saw the horse's breathing steady and its
eyes start to lose their panicked look as Sita's
magic began to calm it.

The rider came running up the road. "Oh
my goodness. Are you all okay?"

"Yes, we're fine," said
Lexi, although she
looked very shaken.

"I don't know
what happened.
Duke has never
reared or galloped
off like that.
Something in the
bushes must have
spooked him."

Mia remembered the flash of movement she had seen and peered into the undergrowth. With the magic running through her, she could see every leaf, every twig, and every branch, but there was nothing unusual. Still, *something* had made the horse rear. Something red and green....

Sita led the horse over. He nuzzled his rider on the arm.

"You silly thing, what was that all about?" his rider said. She gave the girls a relieved look. "I'm glad you're safe. I thought he was going to knock you down," she said to Lexi. "I'm really sorry if he scared you."

"Don't worry," said Lexi. "I'm all right."

Luckily, Mia thought in her head.

The rider said good-bye, mounted, and rode off.

Mia glanced around at the others. "We need to talk."

As soon as they ran into the clearing, the animals appeared.

"What happened?" Bracken said, looking at Mia's face.

Mia hugged him and drew in a deep breath. She felt better now that he was with her. Looking up, she saw that the others were close to their animals, too—Juniper was on Lexi's shoulder, Sita was hugging Willow, and even Sorrel, who was normally so haughty, had jumped onto Violet's lap.

Mia began to tell Bracken about the incident with the horse and the others piped in, too.

"If Mia hadn't yelled at me to jump the other way, that horse would have knocked me down," said Lexi.

Juniper jumped around to her other shoulder in concern. "Do you think someone was trying to hurt you?"

Lexi swallowed. "I suppose it *could* just have been an accident."

Sorrel jumped off Violet's lap. "If a Shade caused that horse to bolt, I'll be able to smell it on the road." She leaped into the bushes.

They waited anxiously until Sorrel came bounding back out of the bushes, her tail puffed up. "A Shade *was* there," she said with a hiss. "The same one. That horse galloping at Lexi was no accident."

"We need to do something!" said Violet.

"I don't want to fight a Shade again," Sita said in a shaky voice.

Willow nuzzled her comfortingly.

"Um… I think I need to tell you something," Mia said. "The three visions I saw in the mirror have all come true, and we now know the accidents all involve the same Shade. Well, I think they're linked and that someone is deliberately trying to hurt people on the gymnastics team."

They all stared at her.

"On the gymnastics team?" echoed Lexi.

"Of course," breathed Violet. "Hannah, Alyssa, and Lexi are all on the gymnastics team."

"But why would someone want to hurt people on the team?" Lexi said.

"Could it be someone on a rival team?" Bracken said.

"No! The teams are competitive, but none of them would want to hurt someone else," said Lexi.

"But someone's responsible for this," said Juniper.

"We have to find out who it is," said Sita.

Violet caught her breath. "Mia—why don't you ask the magic to show you!"

"I can try," said Mia eagerly.

She pulled the mirror out of her pocket and opened her mind to the magic. As it tingled through her, she concentrated hard, like Aunt Carol had told her, and thought, *Show me the person conjuring the Shade that hurt Hannah and Alyssa and tried to hurt Lexi.*

The mirror flickered and then went dark.

Mia blinked. "That's weird."

"What's going on?" asked Sita. "What can you see?"

"Nothing. The mirror just went black. What does it mean, Bracken?"

The fox looked worried. "The person using dark magic may have cast a spell so they can't be seen by magic."

"Oh." Mia's hopes deflated. "Well, how about I try and see the Shade?" she said. "If I ask to see it, maybe we'll find out what object it's trapped in."

"Good idea!" said Violet.

Mia took a breath and focused on the mirror again. *Show me the Shade who made the horse bolt,* she thought.

The darkness faded, and a picture appeared in the mirror. There was an expanse of green lawn, some trees, a bench, and a shed in the distance.

"What can you see?" asked Lexi eagerly.

"A yard," said Mia in surprise.

"Is there anything there that might have a Shade trapped inside it?" asked Bracken.

"No, there's just grass and trees and plants," Mia said.

"There must be something there," said Sorrel impatiently. "Look harder."

"I *am* looking," said Mia in frustration. "I can't see anything."

"Could the Shade be invisible?" suggested Sita.

"No," said Bracken. "Some Shades can move very fast, but they're not invisible."

Violet sighed. "This isn't getting us anywhere."

"It's not Mia's fault!" Lexi said defensively.

"Violet didn't say it was," Sita said quickly. "Why don't you try looking at the accidents? Maybe we can figure out how the Shade caused them," she said to Mia.

Mia hesitated. She hadn't yet managed to look into the past. Could she do it now? She remembered Aunt Carol's advice about needing to really focus. Staring at the mirror and frowning in concentration, she whispered, "Show me Hannah's accident."

A blurry image started to appear in the mirror. Mia peered closer. *Work,* she thought. *Work now.* But the picture only grew more blurry.

"I can't do it!" she told the others. She willed the mirror to show more, but the image remained fuzzy.

Bracken nuzzled her. "Don't worry. Looking into the past is hard."

To Mia's surprise, Sorrel nodded. "The fox is right. Don't feel frustrated, child."

Mia sighed. "Thanks," she said gratefully.

"We'll have to think of some other way to find out what's going on," said Lexi. She glanced at her watch. "I have to go. Mom is meeting me at Violet's soon. I can't be late."

"But what about the Shade?" said Violet.

"It'll have to wait until tomorrow," said Lexi. "We'll have lots of time to try and find out what's going on when we're at Mia's for the sleepover."

"Good idea," said Sita. "Come on. Let's all walk back together. You shouldn't be on your own, Lexi, in case something else happens."

Mia swallowed down her frustration. She didn't want to have to wait until the next day. She wanted to do something right then and there. She'd just have to try even harder, as Aunt Carol had said. Thinking that made her realize that she still hadn't asked Aunt Carol if she had discovered anything. *I'll go and see her on the way home*, Mia decided.

On the way to Aunt Carol's, Mia texted her mom.

> Finished at Violet's. Going 2 c Aunt Carol. Is that OK? M xx

A text quickly buzzed back.

> That's nice of you. I think she's lonely without Grandma Anne. I'll pick you up there. xxx

Mia hurried up the road. This time the

lights were on at Aunt Carol's house, and she was dusting a display of glittering crystals and stones that were on the windowsill in the living room. Spotting Mia through the window, Aunt Carol waved and came to open the front door.

"Mia! Come in."

Mia followed her inside.

"So, what's been going on? Let me get some drinks and cookies, and you can tell me everything," Aunt Carol said. She bustled around, grabbing a tray and glasses.

Soon they were sitting in the living room beside the fireplace. Mia started to tell Aunt Carol everything that had been happening.

"That's awful!" said Aunt Carol, looking shocked when Mia told her about the horse bolting up the road. "Poor Lexi must have been so scared."

"She was. It was a Shade that caused it. Sorrel went back, and she sensed one had been there."

Mia nibbled a cookie. "Have you managed to find out anything, Aunt Carol?"

Aunt Carol sighed. "I'm afraid not. The crystals aren't showing me anything. I just see darkness when I try and look."

Mia felt a rush of disappointment. "That's what happened when I tried to look. Bracken says the person who trapped the Shade must have cast a spell to keep themselves from being seen."

"Yes, that's what I've been thinking, too," said Aunt Carol quickly. "Well, I guess all we can do is keep on trying. This can't be allowed to continue."

"Thank you," said Mia. Just knowing Aunt Carol was trying to help made her feel better.

"Tell me as soon as you discover anything else," said Aunt Carol.

"I will," Mia said.

There was a knock on the door. "That's probably my mom," said Mia.

"No more talking about magic then," said Aunt Carol with a smile. "And I'd better make a fresh pot of tea."

10
THE SLEEPOVER

When Mia got up the next morning, she tried using her magic to see the local gymnastics clubs in her bedroom mirror, to check whether there was anything suspicious going on. But all she saw were teams practicing their routines.

Halfway through the morning, her mom knocked on her door and looked into her room.

Mia hurriedly picked up her phone as if she were writing a message.

"Come on," her mom said. "You've

been shut in here too long. Time to come downstairs. You can help me clean up."

"Okay," said Mia reluctantly.

Her mom shook her head. "You girls and your phones. You're on them way too much."

Mia thought what her mom would say if she told her she hadn't been on her phone, she'd been using magic!

She helped clean up and then got ready for the sleepover. By three o'clock, everything was set. Her bedroom floor was covered with squishy comforters and pillows. She had gone to the store and bought candy for a midnight snack, and her mom had helped her make some toffee. It was cooling downstairs in the kitchen beside a bag of giant fluffy marshmallows for toasting on the bonfire her dad had built in the backyard.

"Make sure you save some marshmallows for me," said Cleo as she came into the kitchen and helped herself to a piece of toffee.

"What time are you babysitting Paige today?" Mia asked.

"I'm going over there now and staying until eight o'clock," said Cleo. "I wish I wasn't. There's a music awards ceremony on TV that I really want to watch. Maybe Paige will watch it with me. Or why don't you come over? You could play with her while I watch it."

"I can't. Lexi, Sita, and Violet will be here any minute," said Mia.

Cleo sighed and grabbed her bag from the

back of the chair. "All right. See you later."

"'Bye!" Mia called as Cleo opened the front door.

"Oh, hi there, Violet," Mia heard Cleo say. "Mia's in the kitchen. Go on in."

Mia went into the hall as Violet came in. She had a spotted blue bag with her. "Hi," Mia said. "Should we take your bag up to my room?"

Violet nodded. As they went upstairs, she whispered to Mia, "Was Aunt Carol able to tell you anything new?"

Mia shook her head. They went into the room and shut the door behind them. "Aunt Carol hasn't been able to find out anything."

Violet dropped her bag on one of the comforters. "I couldn't sleep last night. I kept thinking about everything. Sorrel and I shadow-traveled a little, and tried to see if we could find any other traces of dark magic."

"Did you find anything?" Mia asked eagerly.

"Not much. Sorrel got a strong scent of it up near the main road, but she thinks that might have been from when the Shade tried to hurt Lexi. The scent faded when we traveled farther into town. Have you tried using your magic again?" Violet asked.

"Yes, but looking at people in rival gymnastics clubs hasn't shown me anything useful, and when I try and look back at the accidents to see if I can find any clues, it's really blurry. I wish I could do it. I'm trying to concentrate really hard, just like Aunt Carol told me to, but it's not working."

Violet frowned. "Aunt Carol told you to do that? I find my magic works best when I just relax."

"Aunt Carol said you need to relax when you first connect with your magic, but afterward, it's better if you try to really focus."

"Weird. Maybe her type of magic is different…," Violet said, puzzled.

"I guess so," said Mia.

"Why don't you try what I do? I slowly count down from ten to zero and focus on my breathing, letting everything fade away, then I get this feeling of my magic getting stronger and stronger—it feels like a current of power surging through me," said Violet. "It might work for you, too."

Just then, the doorbell rang. "I bet that's Lexi and Sita," Mia said.

After Mom and Sita's mom had chatted for a few minutes and said their good-byes, the four girls ran upstairs. Mia shut the door, and all the animals appeared.

"Together at last!" said Bracken, jumping around happily as Juniper scampered along Mia's curtain and Willow butted her head affectionately against Sita's legs.

Sorrel stalked into the center of the room. "When you've all finished behaving like three-week-old kittens, can we get started?"

"I hope everyone else on the gymnastics team is okay," said Sita. "Have you heard about anyone else being injured, Lexi?"

"No. The whole team was at training this morning," said Lexi. "And the two replacements. Paige was there with them—she's at the top of the reserve list now, so if anyone else gets injured, she'll be on the team."

"I bet she's happy," said Mia.

Lexi frowned. "It was strange. She was really quiet today."

"I hope she's all right," said Sita.

"Why don't you use magic to check on her,

Mia?" suggested Bracken.

Mia nodded and took her mirror out of her pocket. "Paige," she whispered.

The surface of the mirror flickered, and an image of Paige appeared. It was slightly fuzzy. Remembering what Violet had said, Mia took a breath and counted back from ten, letting the magic flow through her without trying to force it. To her delight, the image grew sharper.

Paige was sitting on a bench in the yard. Her knees were pulled up to her chin, and there were tears rolling down her cheeks. She looked like she was whispering to herself.

"I can see her," Mia told the others. "She's in her yard. She looks really upset."

"Can you see anything else?" Bracken urged.

Mia studied the image intently. She let everything else around her fade away and gradually made out the words that Paige was whispering to herself. "I want it to stop. I'm scared."

Mia's
skin prickled.
She was about to
tell the others when
her eyes caught a movement
behind Paige. The leaves of the
plants quivered as if something was
edging toward the bench.

"There's something in the yard with
Paige!" Mia said anxiously. "It's creeping toward
her."

"What is it?" demanded Violet.

"I can't see," said Mia. "It's hidden by the
shrubs."

"What if it's the Shade?" said Sita.

"We have to go to her!" said Bracken.

"I'll shadow-travel there," said Violet.

"No, we should stay together!" Lexi said.

But Violet was already at the edge of the

room where there was a faint shadow cast
by the afternoon sun. "Come on, Sorrel!"
she cried. The second she stepped into the
shadows, she disappeared, and then Sorrel
vanished, too.

"I can't believe she just did that!" burst out
Lexi. "We have to go, too," she said.

"None of us can shadow-travel," said Sita.

"Maybe not," said Mia, pulling her bedroom
door open. "But we can run!"

11
THE TROUBLESOME GNOME

By the time Mia, Lexi, and Sita reached Paige's house, they were all gasping for breath. Mia's heart thundered in her chest. What were they going to find? What if something had happened to Paige—or Violet? She wished she could call Bracken to her side, but she couldn't risk anyone seeing him.

The three of them raced around the side of the house and into the backyard. To the right there was a small orchard of eight apple trees. In the center of the lawn there was a stone birdbath

and a wooden garden shed with an open door at
the end of the yard. On the far side of the yard
was the bench that Mia had seen Paige sitting
on. But there was no sign of the younger girl
now.

"There's Violet!" said Lexi, pointing into the
orchard.

Violet was standing in
the shadows of the trees
with a rake in her
hands, looking warily
at the bushes.

Mia felt a rush of
relief. Violet was okay.
She ran through the
trees toward Violet
with Lexi and Sita
following her. "Violet!
What's going on?" she
hissed as Violet swung
around to look at her.

"Why did you just go off like that?" said Lexi.

"Because it sounded like Paige was in danger," said Violet.

"Where is Paige?" asked Sita anxiously.

"Inside. Just as I arrived, Cleo came to the French windows and called her in."
Violet continued to scan the yard. "There's something moving in the bushes. It's small, and I caught a glimpse of red and green. I grabbed this rake from the shed in case it attacked me."

"It must be the Shade!" said Mia. "I saw a red and green blur at each of the accidents."

A scuttling sound in the branches above them suddenly interrupted her. They all looked up. "What's that?" said Lexi.

Sita screamed as the branches parted and a pottery face grinned down at them. Its eyes glowed red beneath its bobble hat.

"It's the garden gnome!" cried Lexi.

"A wish was made. It has to come true!" the gnome hissed. "I will hurt one of you!"

"Oh, no, you won't!" said Violet fiercely, lashing out with the rake, trying to hit him.

The gnome cackled and jumped hard on the branch he was standing on.

CRACK! The branch broke and fell, crashing down right onto Lexi and hitting her head. Crying out, she crumpled to the ground.

"Lexi!" Sita gasped.

The gnome jumped down and ran off. Mia and Violet crouched beside Sita. There was a deep gash on Lexi's forehead, but she was trying to sit up.

"Let me help," Sita said. "I can heal you." She gently touched Lexi's head near the cut, and the wound began to close. The pain faded from Lexi's face, but she still looked dazed.

"My head," she said, reaching to touch the place where the wound had been.

"I healed it," said Sita.

"That was amazing, Sita," Violet said.

"Are you all right, Lexi?" Mia asked quickly.

"I think so. I just feel dizzy," said Lexi, blinking. "What happened?"

"The gnome made the branch break," said Mia. "It hit your head."

"So the Shade is in the gnome," said Violet. "It must have been going around hurting people on the gymnastics team. But why?"

"I have no idea. But what's more important is stopping it before it hurts someone else." Lexi tried to stand, but her legs buckled.

"You need to rest," Sita said, catching her.

"Why don't you both stay here while Mia and
I try to find it?" said Violet. "You could wait in
the shed. There are a couple of chairs in there
and a bunch of garden tools you could use to
defend yourselves if the gnome comes back."

"I want to come with you," said Lexi, but
she swayed as she stood up again.

"Lexi, you can't," said Mia.

"Come to the shed with me, Lexi," said Sita.
She looked into Lexi's eyes. "Come on," she
said softly.

The stubbornness slowly faded from Lexi's
face. "Okay," she said obediently.

Mia gave Sita a quick smile—her magic was
getting stronger all the time.

Leaving Sita to help Lexi into the shed, Mia
and Violet ran across the lawn to the house.
"What if it's gone after Paige?" whispered Mia.

There were big French windows that led

from the yard into the house. Mia peered through them and breathed a sigh of relief. Paige was sitting on one of the couches with Cleo. There was no sign of the creepy gnome.

Mia knocked lightly on the window. Paige jumped. Cleo smiled and waved them in. "Hi! Have you come over to see Paige?" she said as they opened the doors.

"Um … yeah," said Mia.

"Good. I think she needs a distraction. Don't you, Paige?"

Paige didn't say anything.

"Are you okay?" Mia asked her, but Paige still didn't speak.

"She's a little upset," Cleo explained. "She was just telling me that a horse almost knocked Lexi over yesterday."

Mia frowned. How did Paige know about that?

"Don't worry, Paige," said Violet. "Lexi's fine."

"But something else might happen to her,"

Paige said fearfully.

"I'm sure it won't," Cleo reassured her.

"But it might!" Paige burst out. "And if it does, it'll be all my fault!" She jumped up and ran out of the room and up the stairs.

Cleo stood up. "I don't know what's the matter with her today," she said. "I've never seen her like this."

Paige's words echoed uneasily in Mia's head. What did she mean? Why did she think it would be her fault?

"Would you like us to talk to her?" Violet offered.

"I should probably do it," said Cleo, glancing longingly at the TV.

"Don't worry. We'll go," said Mia.

"Okay, then," said Cleo, settling back down. "If you need me, give me a shout. Where are Lexi and Sita?" she said, looking around.

"Outside in the yard," said Mia truthfully. "We'll go and see if Paige is okay."

Exchanging looks, she and Violet hurried
out of the room. They heard Cleo turn up
the sound on the TV as they ran up the wide,
sweeping staircase. The house was very big,
with two floors of bedrooms and bathrooms
above the ground floor. The lights were off on
the stairs and landing, and it was very dark and
gloomy. Mia's skin prickled. Light was shining
out from underneath Paige's bedroom door.
They hurried toward it.

Mia knocked. "Can we come in, Paige?"

"Okay." Paige's voice was tearful.

They pushed open the door and went
in. The walls were covered with pictures
of gymnasts. Paige was sitting on her bed,
hugging an old teddy bear.

Mia wished Sita was there—she always
knew what to say when people were upset.
She glanced at Violet, who cleared her throat.

"Um … what's the matter, Paige?" Violet
said.

"I can't tell you," said Paige. She pulled her knees up to her chest and buried her head in them.

Mia went over rather awkwardly and sat down beside her. "What did you mean when you said Lexi would get hurt and it would be all your fault?"

"I meant what I said. It's my fault that Hannah and Alyssa are hurt, and if Lexi gets hurt, that will be my fault, too…." Paige broke off with a sob.

"It isn't your fault. It really isn't," said Mia, patting Paige's shoulder. She looked at Violet, but Violet just shrugged. She was no better than Mia at comforting people.

"It *is* my fault!" Paige burst out. "He told me I was really good at gymnastics and that I should be on the team. He told me he could make my wish come true and I should wish I was on the gymnastics team. I thought it would bring me good luck—I didn't think he'd bring everyone else *bad* luck!"

"Who are you talking about?" Violet asked.

"The garden gnome!"

Mia's eyes met Violet's in shock.

"He can talk," Paige went on with another sob. "I know you won't believe me, but he's a gnome who can grant wishes, and ever since I wished to be on the team, he's been hurting people. He told me today that he'd made a horse gallop at Lexi but it hadn't worked so he was going to try and do something else."

"Oh, Paige," said Mia, her heart thudding.

"I said I wished I'd never made the wish," said Paige. "I said I didn't wish it anymore, but he just laughed and told me that once a wish has been made, it can't be stopped." She looked up. "Do you believe me?"

"Yes, we do—and we're going to help figure it out," said Violet. "Where's the gnome now, Paige?"

"I … I don't know." Paige gulped. "He moves really fast. One minute he's there, the next he isn't."

"We'll find him," said Mia. She gave Paige a hug. "Run downstairs, shut the door, close the curtains, and stay in the living room until we come and find you. Don't say a word to Cleo. Promise?"

Paige nodded. "Promise," she said, her eyes wide.

They ran along the hallway with her. Reaching the staircase, they watched her go

into the warm, bright living room and shut the
door behind her.

Mia took a deep breath. "Are you ready for
some gnome-hunting?" she asked.

Violet's eyes gleamed as they met hers.
"Bring it on!"

12
HUNT FOR THE
WISH SHADE

"So, where do we start looking?" whispered Violet, glancing around the first-floor landing.

"I'm not sure," said Mia.

They moved slowly along the hallway.

Something red and green raced out of a nearby bedroom. It passed them in a blur and scuttled up the staircase that led to the top floor.

"There it is!" gasped Mia.

Violet was already running up the stairs, taking them two at a time. Mia charged after her.

They reached the top and stopped. There
was a long hallway with rooms leading off it,
but no sign of the gnome.

"Bracken!" whispered Mia. "I need you."
There was a shimmer in the air, and suddenly
Bracken was there beside her. Violet whispered
Sorrel's name and the next moment, the
wildcat appeared, too.

"Violet, what's going on?" demanded Sorrel.
"I can smell the Shade everywhere."

The girls explained in hurried whispers,
their eyes darting around the hallway as they
spoke.

"The gnome must have a Wish Shade in it,"
said Bracken, the hackles on his neck rising.
"Wish Shades work on people's worst feelings,
getting them to make wishes and then bringing
them about in horrible ways."

"Paige is really upset," said Mia. "She didn't
mean for all the accidents to happen."

"And now the Shade won't stop until her

wish has been granted," said Sorrel. "We have to find that gnome."

"It came up the stairs. It must be here somewhere," said Mia.

"We'll catch it," Bracken growled. "It's not going to get away."

"For once you and I are in complete agreement, fox," said Sorrel. Her tail fluffed out like a brush, and she prowled forward. Violet moved silently beside her, and Mia and Bracken followed.

Opening her mind, Mia let magic flow into her. Every cell in her body felt as if it was on red alert. Where was the gnome hiding?

A sinister giggle echoed out of a room halfway down the hallway.

Sorrel and Bracken bounded forward, moving as one. They leaped into the room with Violet and Mia hot on their heels.

They were in a spare bedroom with a double bed, wardrobe, and a large window that looked out to the yard. Mia glanced around the room. Her eyes met Violet's. They nodded at each other in silent agreement and edged farther into the room, matching each other step for step. Mia opened the wardrobe while Violet checked inside the drawers.

"Where are you, Shade?" growled Bracken.

The gnome burst out from behind the curtains with a cackle. "Made you look! Made you stare!" he crowed, his eyes glowing red. "Now it's time to give *someone* a scare!" Throwing himself at the bed, he bounced on it and somersaulted over their heads. Sorrel flung herself upward, but her claws

just missed the gnome's head. He landed and
rolled on the floor. Bracken leaped at him,
but the gnome was too fast. He darted out of
the room. Bracken barked in frustration and
chased after the gnome, with Violet, Sorrel
and Mia close behind. He ran into a room
at the end of the hallway, slamming the door
shut behind him.

Violet slowly turned the handle and pushed open the door, revealing a room with a desk and filing cabinets. But the gnome was nowhere to be seen.

Bracken put his nose to the floor as if following a scent and padded over to the open window. He put his paws on the window ledge and looked out. "I think he went out through the window."

Sorrel followed him and sniffed the air. "You're right. He's not here anymore."

"I thought he said he was going to scare us—not run away," said Violet, puzzled. She turned to Mia. "Can you use your magic to find out where he went?"

Mia pulled the mirror out of her pocket and kneeled down on the floor.

"I want to see where the gnome is now," she whispered.

An image appeared in the mirror. It looked like the back of a wooden shed. The gnome was heading toward it, a burning branch in his hand. More branches had been piled behind the shed like a bonfire.

"The gnome's trying to set fire to the shed!" she exclaimed. "He must still be trying to make Paige's wish come true by hurting Lexi. He led us up here because he wanted us out of the way."

"Of course!" gasped Violet. "It's Lexi he's after, not us! We have to stop him!"

They all raced out of the room and down the stairs and out through the kitchen door.

The sun was low in the sky now. The smell of smoke drifted toward them from the fire behind the shed, and Mia could hear the faint crackle of burning branches. Once the fire took hold, it would spread to the wooden sides of the shed.

Violet charged toward the shed. "Sita! Lexi! Get out of there!"

Bracken and Sorrel raced ahead of her.

Bracken leaped for the door handle and tried to turn it with his teeth, but the door wouldn't open.

"It's locked!" he barked.

Mia ran up to the door while Violet ran to a water faucet on the side and started to fill a bucket with water to try and douse the bonfire. Hearing the commotion, Lexi and Sita appeared at the small window.

"I can smell smoke," Sita said. "What's happening?"

"You've got to get out!" Mia shouted frantically. "The shed's going to catch fire any minute!" She started tugging at the bolt that had been pushed across the door on the outside. The bolt was stiff, but she managed to pull it back and yanked the door open.

For a second Mia saw the relief on Sita and Lexi's faces, and then Sita's eyes widened in horror as she looked at something behind Mia.

"The gnome!" she cried.

Mia heard a cackle and felt herself being shoved in the back. Losing her balance, she fell inside the shed. Before she knew what was happening, the door had been slammed shut, and she heard the bolt being pushed back across on the outside.

"Now I've got you! Now you're caught! Now a lesson you'll be taught!" she heard the gnome crowing.

"What's going on?" Lexi demanded, helping Mia to her feet.

Mia registered with relief that Lexi looked completely back to normal. Juniper was jumping around the walls, and Willow was trembling by the door.

"The gnome's trying to burn down the shed," said Mia desperately. "We have to get out of here!" She hammered on the door. "Violet! Unlock the door!" Her heart pounded as the first tendrils of smoke started to fill the shed.

"Look!" said Lexi, pointing out the window. The gnome was in front of the door.

Violet was facing him, hands on hips, the bucket at her feet. "Let my friends out!" she demanded.

"No!" the gnome snickered.

Violet's eyes narrowed. "I command...."

In a flash, the gnome turned his back on her. "I can't see you!"

"She has to be looking into his eyes to be able to command him," said Bracken, his paws on the window ledge.

The gnome said, "I know you want to send me back to the shadows. But I'm having too much fun in the human world to go back there." He paused. "Now, let's think about you, Violet. When this shed burns down, I'll have granted Paige's wish to be on the gymnastics team. Maybe *you* would like some help next." His voice became soft and persuasive. "What could I help you with? Mia, maybe....You *really* wish you could be her, don't you?"

Mia frowned. What was he talking about?

"I don't know what you mean," said Violet, shooting a nervous glance at the shed.

"I can see your thoughts." The gnome moved backward, getting closer to her but being careful not to make eye contact. "Everyone likes Mia, don't they? She's Little Miss Popular. She doesn't even seem to try and *still* people like her. It's not fair, is it? You could be like that, though. One wish and she will get all the bad luck." He gave a sly giggle.

"Now what do you say?" He rubbed his hands together greedily.

"Well … I suppose you do have a point," said Violet.

"No," Mia whispered.

"I mean, it is really tempting," Violet said, wandering back toward the orchard.

The gnome cackled and edged closer still, moving away from the shed door. "I know. All you have to do is make one little wish."

"One wish," echoed Violet. She reached the shadows of the trees and spun around. "I know what I'd like to wish for." She vanished.

The gnome spluttered in shock.

In the blink of an eye, Violet appeared in the shadows of the shed by the door. "I wish for my friends to be free! And, hey, I don't even need your magic to do it!" She pulled back the bolt and opened the door.

Mia, Lexi, and Sita charged out of the shed, the Star Animals at their sides. As they ran, they all drew on their Star Magic. Instantly, Mia could see everything in incredible detail.

"No!" shrieked the gnome, leaping onto the birdbath in the center of the lawn. "I will hurt you!" he screamed, pointing at Lexi. "I will grant Paige's wish!"

"I don't think so!" Juniper said, jumping off Lexi's shoulder and grabbing a fallen apple in his mouth. He scampered up her leg and nudged it into her hand. "Time to hit a real target, Lexi! Knock him off the birdbath!"

Lexi drew back her arm, then chucked the apple at the gnome. It shot through the air with perfect accuracy and hit him square on the forehead. "Bullseye!" she cheered as the gnome lost his balance and fell backward.

There was a cracking noise as he broke into pieces.

A cloud of darkness rose from the shattered pieces of pottery and formed into a tall figure. His nose and chin were pointed, and his eyes glowed red. Ragged clothes hung off his angular body.

"I am free!" he hissed in delight, his voice shivering through the air. As he spoke, his body became more and more solid. "I can go where I want and do as I will. I shall do whatever I like."

Bracken raced toward him. "No, you won't! I'll stop you!"

Mia's heart leaped into her mouth. "Bracken! Come back!"

"Say the words, Violet," said Sorrel, her back arching.

Violet pointed her finger at the Shade. "I command you to…."

"No! I will not be commanded! I will not be sent back!" The Shade started to stride away, but Bracken reached him. With a growl, he bit the Shade's leg and hung on tight. The Shade hissed and swiped down with his sharp claws. With the magic coursing through her, Mia saw where the Shade's hand was going to land an instant before it did. "Bracken! Go left!" she yelled.

Bracken flung himself to the left just in time. The Shade missed

him. Bracken tumbled over onto his back. Mia watched as the Shade lifted its arm to strike the fox. She raced forward. "No! You won't hurt Bracken!"

But Sorrel, Willow, and Juniper were even faster. With two bounds, Sorrel sprang up onto the Shade's back. "Stop right there, Shade!" she hissed, her claws digging in. The Shade howled and swung this way and that, trying to shake her off.

Juniper dashed in front of the Shade's feet, tripping him up. He stumbled to his knees. Willow butted the Shade in the chest with her head, sending him sprawling onto his back.

Lexi was beside him in the blink of an eye. As the Shade started to sit up, she jumped onto his chest, pushing his shoulders back down again. He hissed in fury and arched his back.

"A little help here!" Lexi gasped.

Mia reached the Shade at the same moment Sita did. Flinging themselves down, they each grabbed one of the Shade's bony arms, pinning his hands down.

"No!" he shrieked, thrashing from side to side.

Mia could feel her grip loosening. She couldn't hold on much longer. And then suddenly Violet was there, leaning over the Shade and looking into his red eyes.

"I command you to return to the Shadows!" she said before he could close his eyes.

With a strangled cry, the Shade started to dissolve into a shadow. He twisted and turned as he became smaller and smaller. "This is not the end," he hissed. "She will find ways to bring misery. She will call more of us forth from the Shadows even though one of you has more power than she can dream of!" With a final hiss he faded away to nothing.

There was a moment's silence. "What was that all about?" Violet said.

"I don't know—but we did it!" said Mia, getting to her feet and looking at the ground where the Shade had been. "We sent it back to the Shadows."

Bracken and Juniper raced around in happy circles. Willow bucked, and even Sorrel gave a satisfied meow. "Great job, everyone!" she declared.

"The shed!" exclaimed Sita, looking around and seeing that the branches of the bonfire were burning and that the flames were starting to lick at the wooden sides of the shed. "We have to put out the fire!"

The girls grabbed buckets from inside the shed, and with Lexi running at top speed back and forth between the shed and the water faucet, they emptied bucket after bucket over the flames.

The fire was finally extinguished, leaving the air heavy with the smell of smoke. The shed, thankfully, was unharmed, aside from a few scorch marks around the back.

The girls collapsed on the ground, hugging their animals.

"We fought another Shade," said Mia.

"What do you think he meant," said Violet, "when he said all that stuff about one of us having a lot of power?"

"You must be the one the Shade spoke of, Violet," said Sorrel.

"It said the person who conjured the Shade is a she," said Bracken.

"We need to find her, whoever she is, and stop her," said Juniper.

"Let's worry about that another day," said Lexi. "I've had enough excitement for now. I just want to go and have a sleepover!"

"Me, too," said Violet, with a smile.

Mia got to her feet. "We'd better say good-bye to Paige."

Violet nodded, and she and Mia headed back to the house. Paige was still watching the music awards with Cleo.

"I thought you went home," said Cleo in surprise.

"We're going now," said Mia. "The gnome's gone, Paige."

"Gone? For good?" said Paige eagerly.

Mia and Violet nodded.

"You mean that cute little pottery gnome?" said Cleo. "What happened to it?"

"It got smashed," said Mia.

"Mia! What will Paige's mom and dad say?" Cleo said anxiously.

"Don't worry—they didn't really like it," said Paige. "I think they'll be glad it's gone." She smiled at Mia and Violet in relief. "Thanks!"

"No problem. See you soon." Violet and Mia waved and left.

As they walked around the house to join the others, Mia glanced at Violet. She couldn't help thinking about what the gnome had said when she had been locked in the shed with Lexi and Sita. Surely Violet wasn't really jealous of her, was she?

Violet saw her glance. "What?" she said warily.

"The gnome said some stuff when I was in the shed. You're not really jealous of me, are you?"

Violet's cheeks flushed bright red. "No," she said, avoiding Mia's gaze. "Of course not."

Mia's eyes widened. Violet's blush gave her away even though she was denying it. But why? She was so clever.

"So what if you're popular and everyone likes you," Violet went on defensively. "That's you. I'm me. I'm fine with it."

Mia didn't know what to say. She swallowed. "Oh. Okay. Well, just so you know … I'm … I'm glad you became a Star Friend, too." The words came out in a rush. Her mind flashed back to being in the house with Violet and Sorrel, tracking down the gnome, and she realized she meant it. "Thank you for helping me with my magic. That stuff you said about relaxing really worked and … well, it's been fun doing stuff together today."

Their eyes met. Violet's face softened. "It has been, hasn't it? We make a good team. Bracken and Sorrel do, too—only don't tell Sorrel I said that," she added.

"No way," said Mia. "I wouldn't dare."

They exchanged grins and continued on in silence. Mia's steps felt suddenly lighter. Maybe she and Violet could be friends again after all— real friends.

Lexi and Sita were waiting for them by the trampoline. Mia held up her hand, and they high-fived her. "We did it," she said. "We sent another Shade back to the Shadows."

Lexi linked arms with her. "It's sleepover time."

"Time to toast marshmallows on the bonfire," said Violet.

"And eat toffee," said Mia.

"And no need to worry about fighting any more Shades tonight," added Sita happily.

A couple of hours later, they were all snuggled up in Mia's room with their animals lying beside them or cuddled in their arms. They were full of marshmallows and candy.

"It's been such a scary few days." Sita sighed. "I'm glad it's over and no one else is going to get hurt."

"For now," said Sorrel darkly. "The person who trapped the Shade is still out there somewhere. We should be looking for her."

Bracken made a grumbling noise in his throat. "One night off isn't going to hurt us."

Sorrel looked at him dryly. "It's not us I'm worried about."

Violet petted her. "It's all right, Sorrel. We'll start trying to find the person who conjured the Shade tomorrow."

"I wonder if Paige's family was given the gnome on purpose," Sita said.

They were all silent for a moment. It was horrible to think of someone deliberately setting out to bring misery to Paige or her family.

"Whoever trapped the Shade must be really evil," said Lexi with a shiver.

"But one of us is more powerful," Violet reminded them. "That's what the Shade said."

"I'm sure it's you," purred Sorrel. "After all, you're the Spirit Speaker."

"I think it's Mia," said Bracken loyally. "Her magic is getting stronger all the time. Soon she'll be able to look into the past and even see into people's thoughts."

"Useful, I agree," said Sorrel. "But she's not as powerful as Violet."

"It could be Lexi," put in Juniper, snuggling his head under Lexi's chin.

"Yep, with my deadly apple-throwing ability," said Lexi with a grin.

"As long as it's not me," said Sita. "I don't want to be powerful. I just want to heal people and make them better."

Mia thought about it. She liked the thought
of being really powerful and being able to scare
people who were using dark magic. Which
of them was it? As she considered it, a wave
of tiredness suddenly swept over her, and she
yawned. "Should we turn off the light?"

The others all nodded sleepily.

"'Night, everyone," Mia whispered.

"'Night," came the sighs back.

Bracken snuggled up on Mia's chest and
licked the tip of her nose. She smiled and
kissed the soft spot between his ears. She felt
safe and warm and happy. She was surrounded
by her best friends with Bracken by her side.
There was no doubt they were going to have
more excitement, but for now, fighting evil and
doing magic could wait until another day.

"'Night, Bracken," she whispered into his ear.

Snuffling contentedly, he snuggled closer
into her arms.

About the Author

Linda Chapman is the best-selling author of more than 200 books. The biggest compliment she can have is for a child to tell her he or she became a reader after reading one of her books. She lives in a cottage with a tower in Leicestershire, England, with her husband, three children, three dogs, and three ponies. When she's not writing, Linda likes to ride, read, and visit schools and libraries to talk to people about writing.

About the Illustrator

Lucy Fleming has been an avid doodler and bookworm since early childhood. Drawing always seemed like so much fun, but she never dreamed it could be a full-time job! She lives and works in a small town in England with her partner and a little black cat. When not at her desk, she likes nothing more than to be outdoors in the sunshine with a cup of hot tea.